A is for

ANNABELLE

A is for ANNABELLE

A DOLL'S ALPHABET

Tasha Tudor

Aladdin Paperbacks

New York   London   Toronto   Sydney

First Aladdin Paperbacks edition June 2004

Copyright 1954 by Oxford University Press
Copyright renewed © 1982 by Corgi Cottage, L.L.C.

ALADDIN PAPERBACKS
An imprint of Simon & Schuster
Children's Publishing Division
1230 Avenue of the Americas
New York, NY 10020

Also available in a Simon & Schuster Books for Young Readers hardcover edition.

Manufactured in China
2 4 6 8 10 9 7 5 3 1

Library of Congress Control Number 00-109523
ISBN 0-689-82845-4 (hc)
ISBN 0-689-86996-7 (Aladdin pbk.)

To dearest muff and Aunt Middle Mary

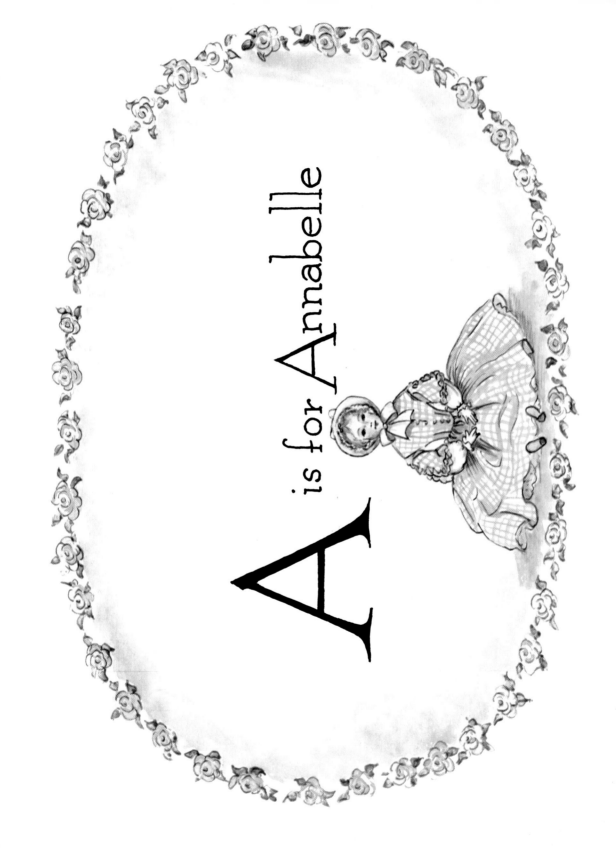

A is for Annabelle

Grandmother's doll

B for her Box

on the chest in the hall

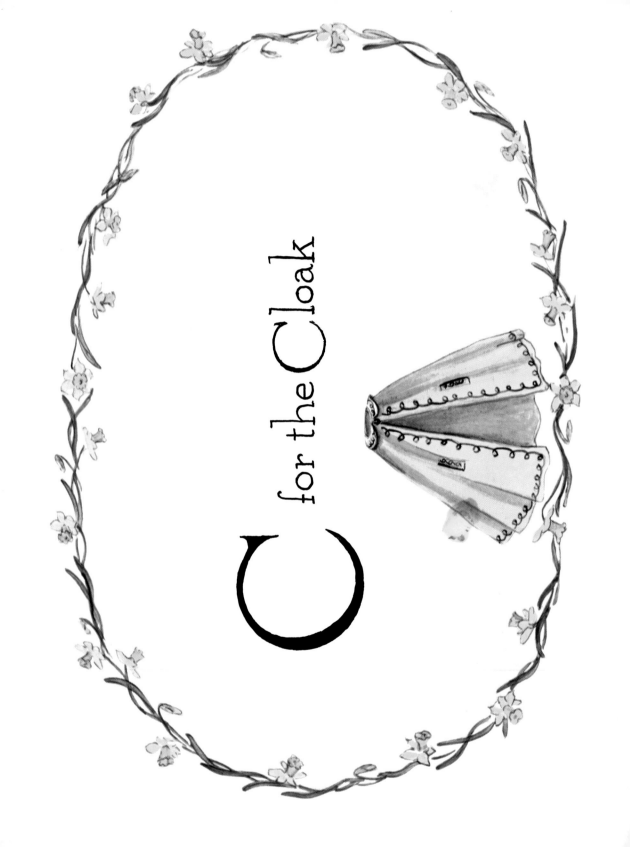

C for the Cloak

we take out with care

D for the Dresses

we want her to wear

E for her Earrings

so quaint and so small

F for her Fan

to use at the ball

G for her Gloves

made of fine leather

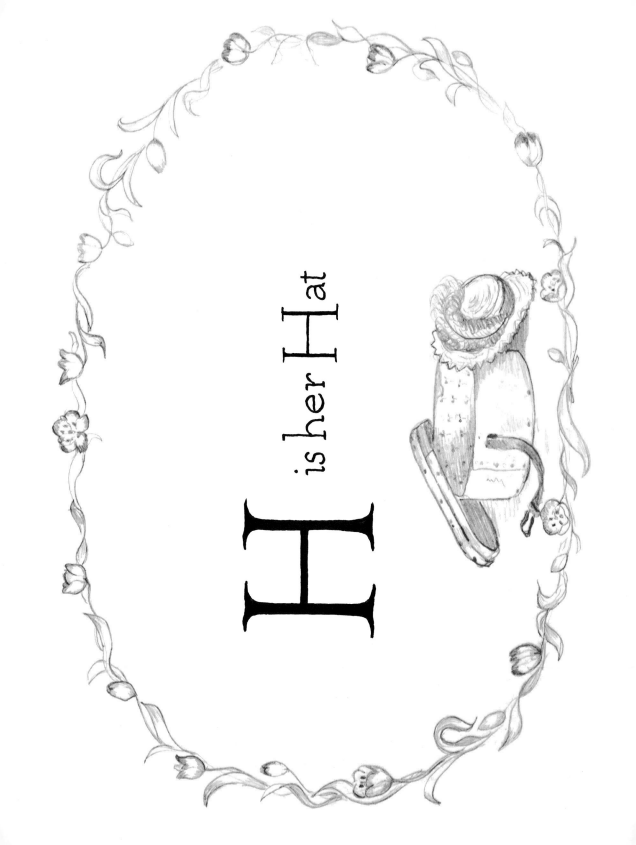

H is her Hat

with an elegant feather

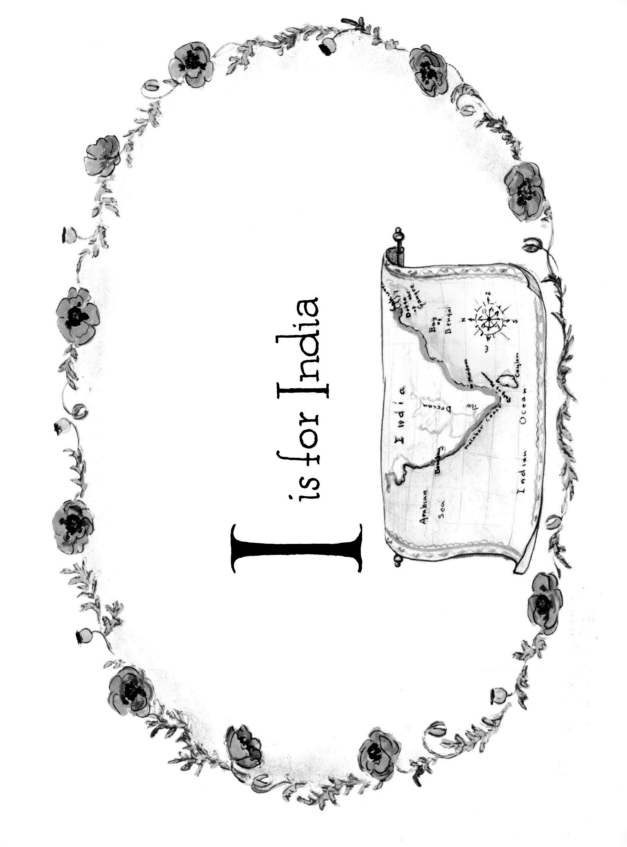

I is for India

whence came her shawl

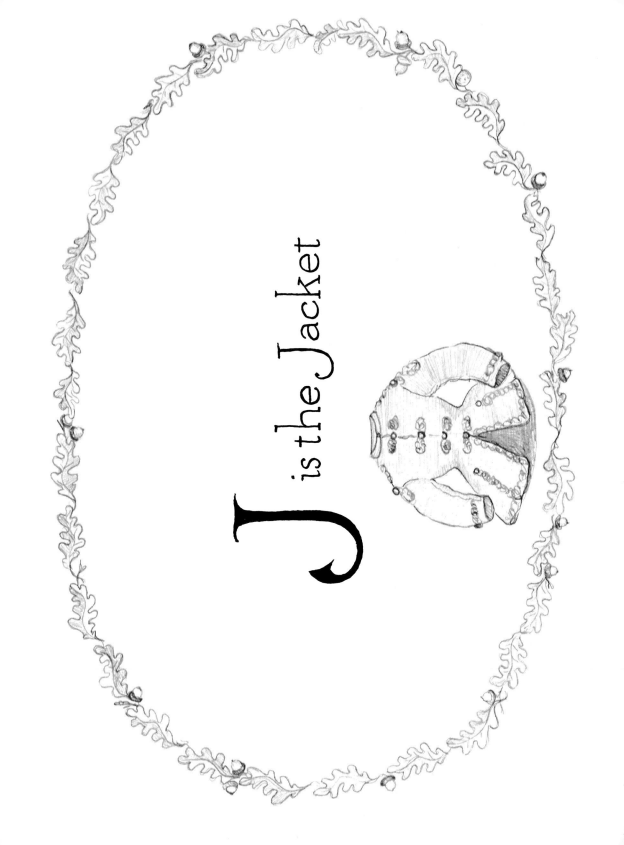

J is the Jacket

she wears in the fall

K is for Kerchiefs

both frilly and plain

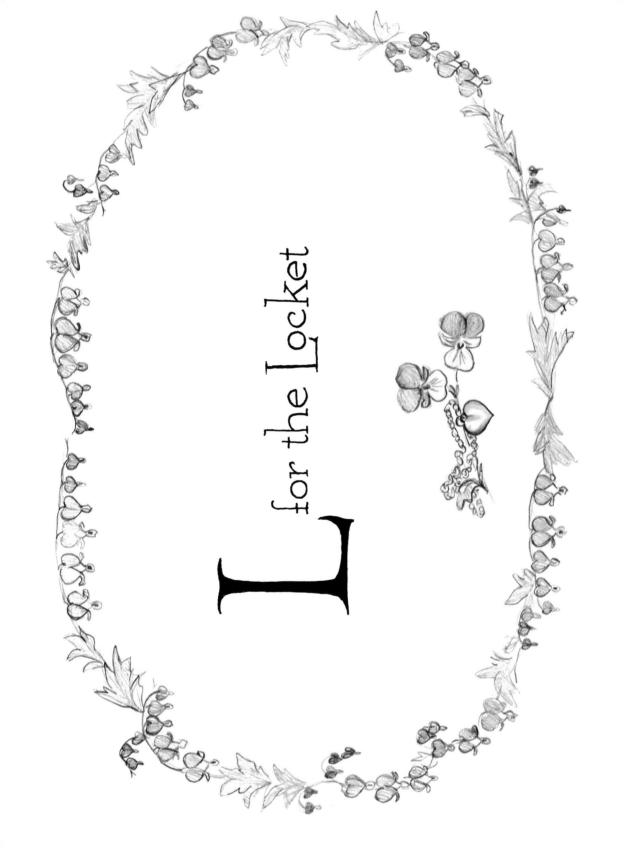

L for the Locket

she wears on a chain

M is her Muff

so warm and so cosy

N is a Nosegay

a bright fragrant posy

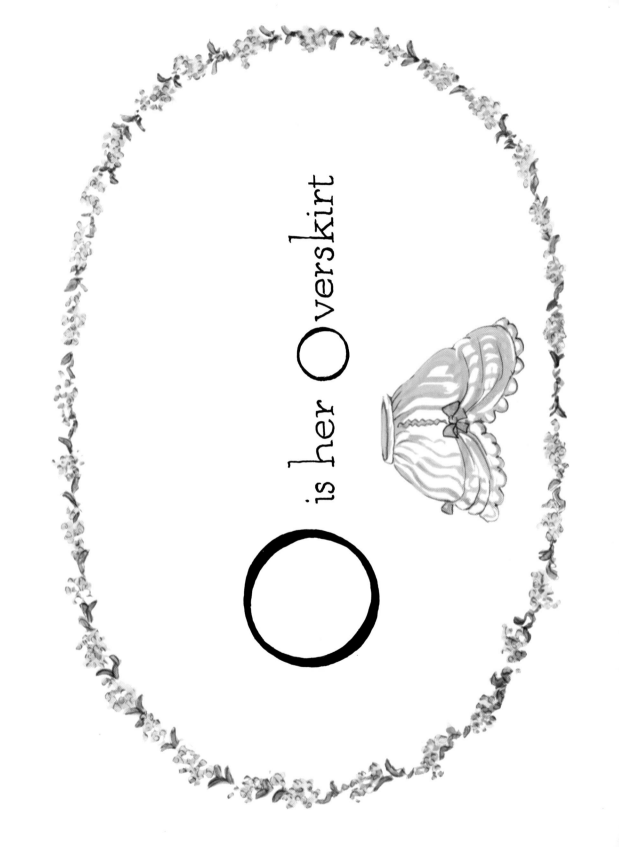

O is her Overskirt

worn with such grace

P for her Parasol

all trimmed with lace

Q is the Quilt

which covers her bed

R for the Ribbons

she ties 'round her head

S for her Slippers

to wear at the dance

T for her Tippet

the latest from France

U for Umbrella

with jethandle on it

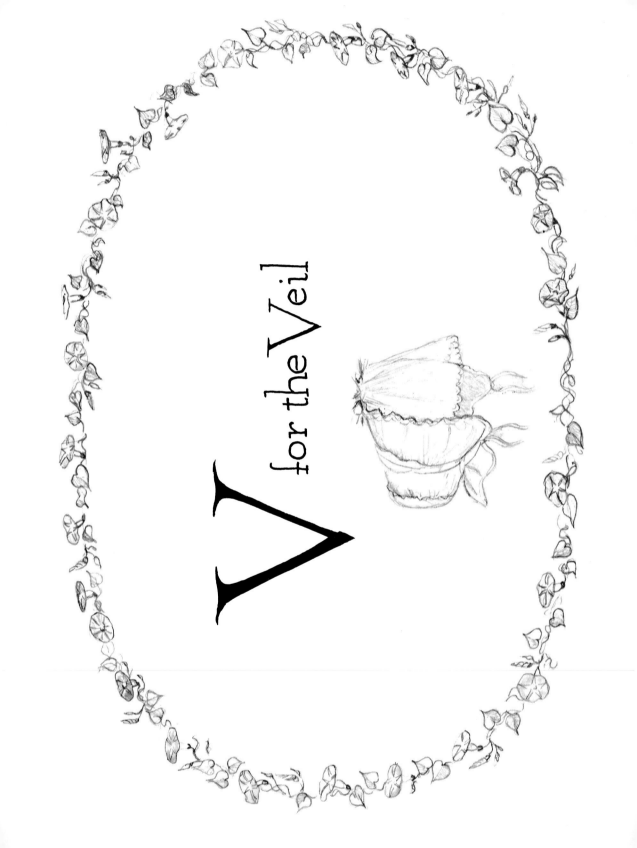

V for the Veil

she wears with her bonnet

W —her Watch

to tell her the time

X is the letter

X is for Xerxes
The King

for which I've no rhyme

Y is the Yarn

her stockings to mend

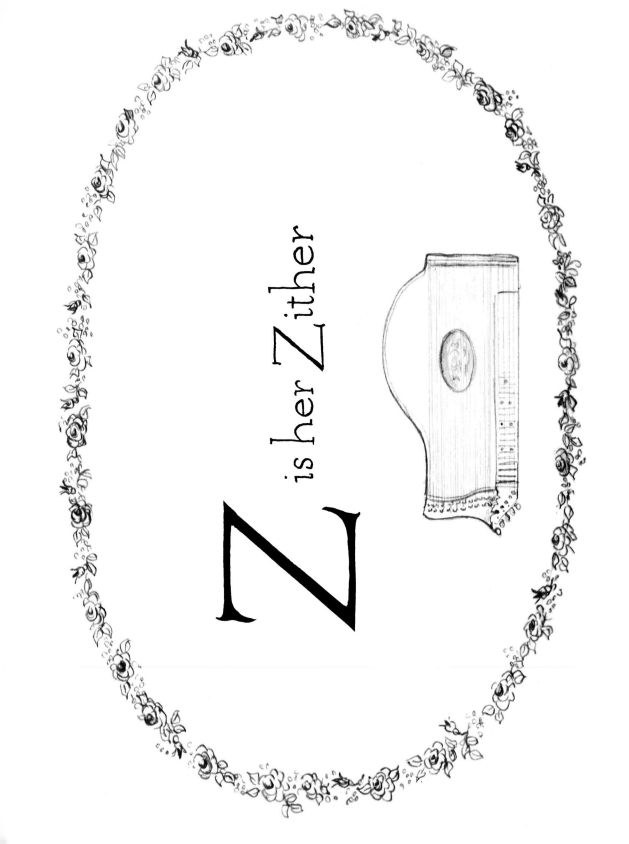

Z is her Zither

and this is the end.